THE LETTER JESTERS

THE LETTER

JeSTeRS

Cathryn Falwell

TICKNOR & FIELDS
Books for Young Readers

NEW YORK 1994

Published
by
Ticknor & Fields
Books for Young Readers
A Houghton Mifflin company
215 Park Avenue South
NEW YORK, NY 10003

Copyright © 1994 by Cathryn Falwell

Manufactured in Singapore
Book Design
by
Cathryn Falwell
The illustrations are
CUT PAPER,
reproduced
in full color
TWP 10 9 8 7 6 5 4 3 2 1

Library of Congress
Cataloging-in-Publication Data
Falwell, Cathryn.
The letter jesters / by Cathryn Falwell.
p. cm.
ISBN 0-395-66898-0
1. Type and type-founding—Juvenile literature. [1. Printing—
Specimens.] 1. Title.
Z250.F196   1994   93-22739
CIP
AC

WITH THANKS TO:
Marshall Lee,
Norma Jean Sawicki,
Julie Amper,
David Saylor,
Anthony Pratt,
Anthony Terenzio,
Lois Sabatino,
William Wondriska,
and Peter Mirkin
*There are many types
and many faces.*

CAST:
Alfonzo,
Bette,
and
Typo,
the letter dog.

THIS
BOOK
is
dedicated
TO
LISA
GARY

JON
...characters
with style!

everywhere!

GO
3
MISS
1
TURN
FREE
SPACE!
ROLL
AGAIN
BACK

STOP

CIRCUS
MAY
17-28

News

ALEXANDER WINS!

The votes are in
and the results

When asked how
he felt about the

Weather:
Sunny today and
mild, high 74-76°

There are many

sizes

AAAA A A A A

and many

styles.

AAAAAAAAAAAA

Each style
is called a

TYPE

FACE.

There are
hundreds of typefaces.
Here are some of them:

Aster	**Broadway**	Gill Sans
Aster Italic	Caledonia	*Gill Sans Italic*
Aster Bold	Centaur	**Gill Sans Bold**
Avant Garde	**Cheltenham Bold**	**GOLD RUSH**
BALLOON	Cloister Black	**Gorilla**
Bamboo	Confetti	*Goudy Cursive*
BANK NOTE	**Futura Black**	Goudy Mediaeval
Bank Script	GALLIA	**Goudy Text**
Barnum P.T.	**Gamma**	**Harry Obese**
Baskerville	Garamond Light	Harry Thin
Baskerville Italic	**Garamond Book**	Helvetica Thin
Blippo Black	GAZETTE	Helvetica
Bodoni Open	**Gibbons**	*Helvetica Italic Outline*

Jester

Legend

MACHINE BOLD

MARBLEHEART

Optima

Orbit-B

Palatino

Palatino Italic

Stradivarius

THUNDERBIRD

Tiffany Heavy

Times Roman

Times Roman Italic

Times Roman Bold

TOO MUCH SHADOW

UNCLE SAM

Wedding Text

Wellington

Western

Willow

Woodstock

Yankee

Zachery

Zingo

Each typeface has a name. Often typefaces are named for the way they look:

STENCIL

noodles

BABY TEETH

or for the people who designed them:

Bodoni

Caslon

Janson

Each of the letters,
numerals, punctuation
marks, and symbols
in a typeface is
called a character.

Here are all the
characters in the
typeface called
Helvetica:

abcdefghijklm
nopqrstuvwxyz
ABCDEFGHI
JKLMNOPQR
STUVWXYZ
1234567890&
$%.,:;!?#+=*()"

The arrangement of characters into words and lines is called typesetting. All characters and spaces in typesetting are measured in points.

A
10 point
A
18 point
A
36 point
A
48 point
A
72 point

This sentence is set in 18-point Garamond Light type.

Typefaces can have variations, too.

Roman

Roman

Roman

Roman

Our alphabet comes from the beautiful, straight letters carved into stone by the ancient Romans.

Characters that stand up straight are called roman.

Italic

Italic

Italic

Italic

An Italian printer, Aldus Manutius, designed the italic style five hundred years ago.

Characters that slant to the right are called italic.

Characters
that look
thin and
delicate
are called
light.

Light

Light

Light

Light

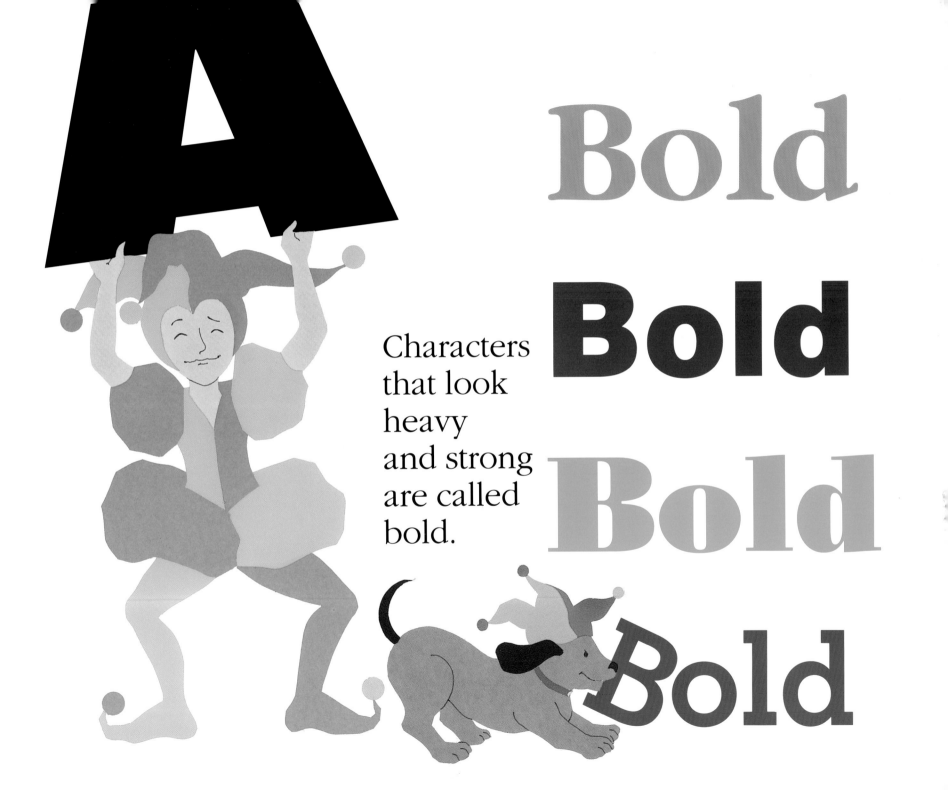

A

Characters that look heavy and strong are called bold.

Bold

Bold

Bold

Bold

The small strokes at the ends of some characters are called serifs. They look like little feet.

The word serif comes from an old Dutch word meaning "dash" or "line."

square: **serif**

rounded: **serif**

pointed: serif

ERIF

Sans

Typefaces without serifs are called sans serif.

flat: **sans**

rounded: **sans**

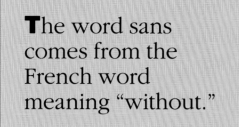

serif

Capital letters
are called

UPPER

Letters were carved
at the top of stone
columns by the ancient
Romans. The top area
of a column is called
the capital.

ABCDEFGHIJKL

Long ago, type characters were made individually, then put together to form words and sentences. These type letters were first made from wood, and later, from metal. The type was then rolled with ink and printed onto paper.

CASE.

MNOPQRSTUVWXYZ

Small letters
are called

lower

a b c d e f g h i j k l m n

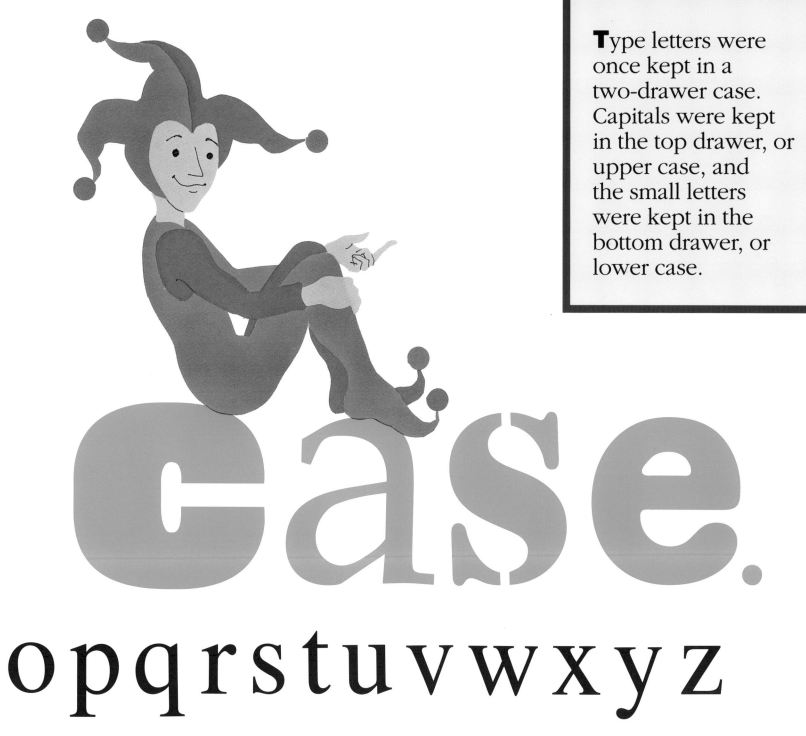

Type letters were once kept in a two-drawer case. Capitals were kept in the top drawer, or upper case, and the small letters were kept in the bottom drawer, or lower case.

case.

opqrstuvwxyz

Typefaces are chosen
for the way they make

WORDS

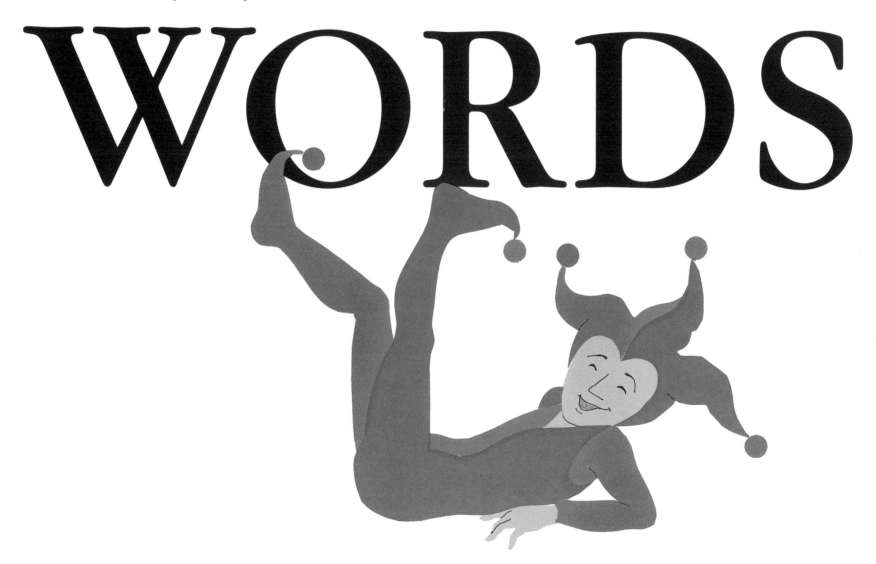

LOOK.

The art of using type is called typography.

Each typeface
can have a
different look
and can express a
different feeling:

dog

dog

DOG

DOG

dog

DOG

SOME

ARE

plain

Some ARE Fancy

some
ARE
FAT

SOME

Are

THIN

SOME

are

Serious

and

SOME

ARE

PLAYFUL

Different typefaces
can produce
different responses
to the same word.

Hundreds of
typefaces,
thousands of
words,

words

made

of

Letters...

letters are
EVERYWHERE!

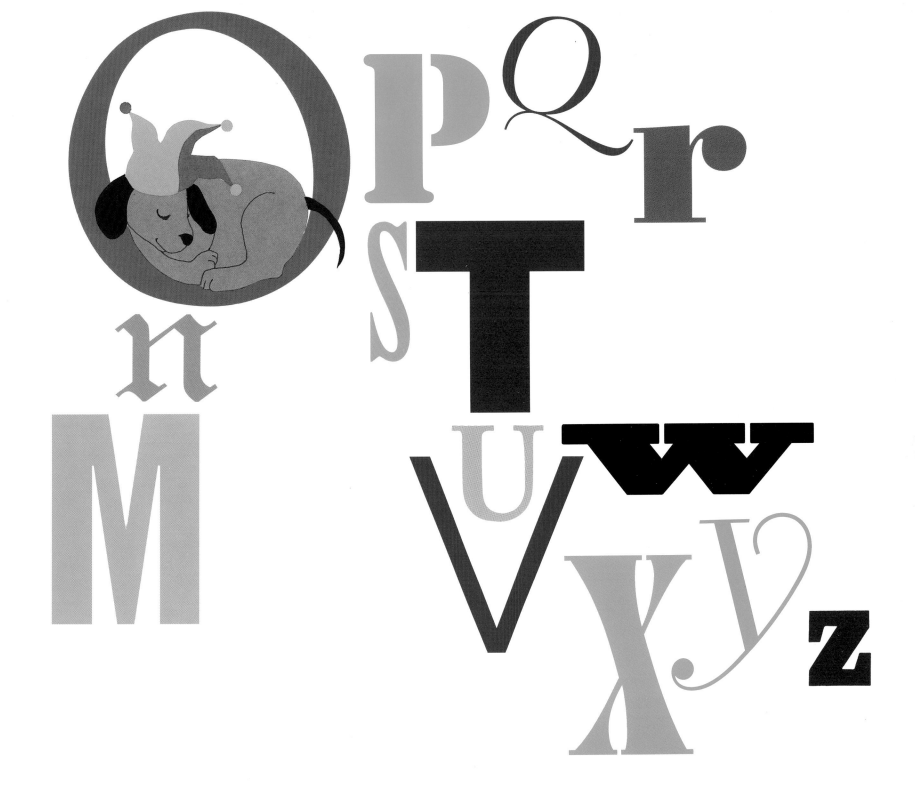